P9-CWE-614

Dear Parent,

When baseball is a boy's greatest passion, having to take piano lessons is not much fun! The only person who understands how Sonny feels is his tango-dancing grandmother Hannah. Thanks to Nana Hannah, Sonny learns to play the piano and still play baseball.

This cleverly written story delivers its message without a lot of preaching. Illustrator Diana Bluthenthal has a light, comic touch and a keen sense of color. The story and art in this new book are a wonderful combination for story time.

Happy reading,

Fritz J. Luecke

Fritz J. Luecke
Editorial Director
Weekly Reader Book Club

Weekly Reader Children's Book Club Presents

Nana Hannah's Piano

BARBARA BOTTNER

ILLUSTRATED BY DIANA CAIN BLUTHENTHAL

G. P. PUTNAM'S SONS · NEW YORK

Special thanks to Alice Bregman and Arthur Levine.—BB

This book is a presentation of Newfield Publications, Inc.
For information about Newfield Publications' book clubs for children
write to: **Newfield Publications, Inc.,** 4343 Equity Drive, Columbus, Ohio 43228

Published by arrangement with G. P. Putnam's Sons, a division of The Putnam & Grosset Group.
Newfield Publications is a federally registered trademark of Newfield Publications, Inc.
Weekly Reader is a federally registered trademark of Weekly Reader Corporation.

1997 edition

Designed by Gunta Alexander. Text set in Gamma Book.
The art was created in gouache and ink on watercolor paper.

Library of Congress Cataloging-in-Publication Data
Bottner, Barbara. Nana Hannah's piano / by Barbara Bottner; illustrated by Diana Cain Bluthenthal.
p. cm. Summary: When a young boy goes to stay with his grandmother, who has twisted her ankle,
he teaches her about baseball and she inspires him to enjoy playing the piano.
[1. Grandmothers—Fiction. 2. Piano—Fiction. 3. Baseball—Fiction.] I. Bluthenthal, Diana Cain, ill.
II. Title. PZ7.B6586Nan 1996 [E]—dc20 94-39159 CIP AC ISBN 0-399-22656-7

For my stepson Geoffrey,
and for Roz, who dances a divine tango. —BB

For my husband, my parents, BB,
and the spirit of Nana in all of us,
with love. —DB

After school, when I want to be at softball practice,
I have to sit down at the piano instead.

I'm not a musician. I'm a first baseman. I want to play in Little League.

My piano teacher has dirty fingernails. She bangs
the keys and tells me I'm hopeless.

I beg my mother to let me stop taking lessons. She tells
me we don't have quitters in this family.

"I'm not a quitter," I say. "I'm an infielder without an
infield."

The only person who understands is my grandmother Hannah, who lives next door. On Fridays I bring her potato dumplings before she goes to her tango class at the Rhapsody Ballroom.

"Sonny, you'll be great at whatever you do," she says.
"Like I am. You should see me dance."

But last Friday she twisted her ankle. That's why I came
to stay with her for a whole week.
"Look at this silly old leg," she says.

"Your cane reminds me of a baseball bat." I show her
how to hit a grounder past shortstop.

"Very interesting, but nothing like the tango."

I wish I could do something to make her feel better.
Over breakfast I demonstrate how to catch a fly ball.
Nana says that move looks a *little* bit like the tango.

Tonight we watch the opening of the World Series.

The Yankees cream the Pirates. Nana Hannah cheers
because she once lived in New York. I'm a Pirates fan.

Afterwards she asks me to help her over to the piano.

Nana's playing makes me forget that my team lost.

"I guess when it comes to music, you either have it or you don't," I tell Nana. She doesn't say anything.

The next morning, while Nana does her exercises, I stretch
my fingers and play a few notes. For a minute I forget that
I hate being near the piano.

Nana Hannah wobbles into the living room. "You have a nice touch," she says.

"What I'm good at is fly balls." I hop down from the bench.

So are the Pirates. That night the Yankees lose. This puts my Nana in a grumpy mood. "What can I do to cheer you up?" I ask.

"You'll think of something," she says, and goes to bed.

Maybe if I could play *one* song for Nana, I could make her forget how badly her leg hurts. I find "Take Me Out to the Ballgame" in an old songbook. I end up trying to get the left-hand chords, and before I know it, it's very late.

The next day I'm tired. My practice team
yells at me when I miss an easy out.

When it gets dark, I sit down at the baby grand and put both hands on the keys. I play very slowly.

Nana looks in and smiles. She's nothing like my
piano teacher.

I stay with my grandma for the rest of the week. Her leg is getting a little better. So am I—I play the piano every day, mostly when Nana goes out to the porch to listen to her tango station.

GAME	1	2	3	4	5	6	7
PIRATES		✓	✓			✓	
YANKEES	✓			✓	✓		

The Series is tied.

On Saturday Nana Hannah takes a walk with a neighbor. I should be out fielding ground balls but I get an urge to sit down and play the stupid piano.

I don't hear Nana tiptoe inside because she isn't making noise with her cane. She doesn't need it anymore!

When I am done, she claps.

"Gotta go. The guys are waiting."

"Let me hear some more!" Nana sits next to me
on the bench.

So I do a chorus from "Take Me Out to the Ballgame."
Nana teaches me the rest of it in a four-hand duet.

Outside, the pitcher and the third baseman go wild. They didn't know I could play the piano.

The Pirates won the Series, but Nana says the Yankees are like her: they'll be back and better than ever!

I'm trying out for the Little League soon. I have a new piano teacher who lives next door and likes potato dumplings.

At the end of my lesson we dance the tango. We make a great team.